—— Anna Sewell ——

BLACK BEAUTY

Published in this edition 1997 by Peter Haddock Ltd,
Pinfold Lane, Bridlington, East Yorkshire YO16 5BT

© 1997 this arrangement, text and illustrations,
Geddes & Grosset Ltd, David Dale House,
New Lanark, Scotland

Illustrated by John Marshall

ISBN 0 7105 1023 3

Printed and bound in France
   by Maury Eurolivres

10 9 8 7 6 5 4 3 2 1

Contents

To the Reader

When you have seen and enjoyed a film or TV programme that has been made from a famous book, you may decide to read the book.

Then what happens? You get the book and, it's more than likely, you get a shock as well! You turn ten or twenty pages, and nothing seems to *happen*. Where are all the lively people and exciting incidents? When, you say, will the author get down to telling the story? In the end you will probably throw the book aside and give it up. Now, why is that?

Well, perhaps the author was writing for adults and not for children. Perhaps the book was written a long time ago, when people had more time for reading and liked nothing better than a book that would keep them entertained for weeks.

We think differently today. That's why some of these wonderful books have been retold for you. If you enjoy them in this shorter form, then when you are older you will go back to the original books and enjoy all the more the stories they have to tell.

About the Author

Anna Sewell was born in Yarmouth in England in 1820, the daughter of Isaac and Mary Sewell. She was an invalid for much of her life and died at Old Catton in Norfolk in 1878.

Black Beauty was published in 1877 and is one of the most famous animal stories ever told. It is set in a period when horses and other animals were often very harshly and cruelly treated, and Anna Sewell's book was important in drawing attention to animal welfare issues.

Black Beauty

In my time I have known many owners – some thoughtless and cruel, others kind and loving . I have pulled fine carriages and poor wagons. I have saved lives and my own life has been saved.
This is my story.

CHAPTER ONE
My First Home

The first place I can remember was a large pleasant meadow with a pond to drink from and trees to give shade when it was sunny. There was a brook at one end and beyond it a steep bank.

When I was young I drank my mother's milk as I could not yet eat grass.

In the daytime I frolicked in the field by her side or played with the other six colts and sometimes our play got very rough.

During the spring and summer when it was warm, we slept outside, me lying close to my mother. In the late autumn and winter when it turned cold, we slept in a warm shed near Farmer Grey's house.

Farmer Grey was our master. He was a kind man who called my mother, Duchess. And because I was dull black, he called me, Darkie.

When I was old enough to eat grass, my mother went to work on the farm or taking the farmer and his wife to market in his little gig, but she always came back in the evening.

One day I was playing with my friends when my mother returned from work. As soon as she saw how rough our games were she whinnied for me to come to her. "Beauty," she said, "you shouldn't play boisterous games like that. Your friends are good colts but they haven't yet learned good manners. You come from a very good family: your father won an important race at Newmarket two years running and your grandmother was the sweetest tempered horse in the world. I hope you grow up to be as gentle and good as she."

I nodded my head.

"And when you are older, always do your work with a good will, lift your feet up well when you trot and never, ever, bite or kick."

I promised my mother I would remember her words for as long as I lived, even though it was difficult to be good when Dick, the ploughboy, came to our field to

pick blackberries. He would soon grow bored, and to amuse himself he would throw stones at me and the other colts to make us gallop round the meadow. We were fast enough to dodge most of the stones, but when they hit their target it hurt.

One day when Dick was doing this, Farmer Grey came into the field and saw what he was up to.

He was furious. He thrust some money into the boy's hand and said, "Here take this and get out. I never want to see you on the farm again."

And we never saw the ploughboy from that day on.

* * *

One day, just before I was two and was still running free in the field with my friends, we heard the hounds baying.

"It's the hunt," one of my friends cried. "They've scented a hare."

As he spoke, a terrified hare lopped across the stream and streaked down the field. A few moments later a pack of ferocious hounds crashed down the bank, followed by seven or eight horsemen.

They thundered across the field, and I was so excited I was desperate to gallop after them. But as I went to follow, one of the horses came tumbling to the ground as it tried to clear the hedge between our field and the plantation beyond.

The young man in the saddle was thrown off and lay where he fell, quite still. His horse tried to get to its feet, but slumped to the ground obviously in great pain.

The other riders dismounted. "It's young Gordon, the squire's son," I heard one of them say. "I think his neck is broken."

"And that's Rob Roy, an old friend of mine," said my mother, nodding at the stricken horse. "He's broken his leg by the look of him."

As we stood watching, one of the men pulled out a gun and pointed it at Rob Roy. There was a loud flash and then a bang. Rob Roy stopped struggling and never moved again.

A few days later we heard the church bells toll and when we looked over the hedge we saw a line of black-draped carriages all drawn by black horses with black plumes on their heads, heading for the church.

There was a long, wooden box on the front carriage.

My mother looked at it, shook her head and said sadly, "A fine horse and a fine young man both killed all for one little hare."

And she was so troubled that for the rest of the time I was in the meadow with her, my mother never went to the part of the field where Rob Roy and the young man had both died.

CHAPTER TWO
I am Broken In

As I got older I became quite handsome. My coat took on a deep lustre and became shiny and black all over apart from one foot which was white, a white star on my forehead and a tiny patch of white on my back.

Several people wanted to buy me, but my master refused to sell me until I was four because he believed that colts should not work like grown horses.

And so, just after I had turned four, he began to break me in, to get me used to the tack I would have to wear now I was grown up and would be expected to carry a rider, pull a carriage or do whatever my master wanted me to do, no matter how tired or hungry.

I was very proud when I heard him say to a friend that because he was so fond of me, he would trust no one else to do this. "I would hate him to be frightened or hurt," he said.

The worst part was having to wear a bit and bridle, the piece of metal that horses have in their mouths and the leather straps attached to it.

I had seen them before, of course, as my mother always

wore them when she went out but even so, it is difficult
to tell how sore it was having the metal bit pushed into
your mouth and held there by a strap. But my master
did it as gently as he could and fed me handfuls of oats
to reward me for my pains.

And when I was used to it, he patted me and said, "Good
boy," over and over again.

Once I was accustomed to the bit and bridle, I was
saddled, and once reins had been attached to the bridle
my master walked me round the meadow every morning for a week or two.

And then one day, he climbed on my back and although
he was quite heavy, I was soon trotting round the field,
turning to the left or right whenever he pulled the reins
to that one side or the other.

It felt strange, but I was very proud of myself.

The very next day, he took me to the blacksmith who
nailed a curved piece of iron onto each of my hooves.
They made my feet feel stiff for a while, but like the bit,
bridle, reins and saddle I soon got used to them.

Then I was taught to wear a harness, a stiff heavy collar that went round my neck, and blinkers, pieces of
leather fixed to the bridle against my eyes so that I could
only see straight ahead.

I bore everything with great patience, but I almost lost
my temper when my master fitted me with a scrupper, a

stiff strap under my tail. It was so uncomfortable that had anyone else put this on me I would have kicked him, but I would never have kicked my master for he had been so kind to me

Now I was ready to pull a cart or carriage and often went out in a double harness with my mother who showed me how go better than a strange horse would have.

During the time I was being broken in, my master sent me for a two weeks to a neighbouring farmer who had a field which was skirted on one side by a railway. I had never seen a train before, and when one roared past, smoke puffing from its stack, I was terrified, but I soon became as accustomed to them as the cows and sheep with whom I shared the field.

One day as we trotted along side by side, my mother said to me, "There are many different kinds of men in the world. Some are as good and kind as our master, but others are bad and cruel. But no matter what kind of master you end up with, I hope you always do you best to keep up your good name."

I was old enough by now to realise that my mother was telling me this because it was time for me to be sold

Chapter Three
I Go to Birtwick Park

Shortly afterwards I was sold to Squire Gordon, the man whose son had been killed during the hunt. The squire and his family lived at Birtwick Park, a fine house that stood in the middle of a large estate.

After Farmer Grey had bid me a fond farewell and I had said goodbye to my mother, I was taken from the farm to the Park where I was led to the stables, a large block that had room for many horses.

The squire led me to a loose box lined with clean, fresh hay, and after he had given me some sweet oats, patted me and left me to settle in.

I was glad that horses kept in loose boxes are not tied up but are free to do what they please. After I had eaten, I looked around my stall and into the one beyond.

"How do you do," I said to the pretty, but fat, grey pony tethered there. "What is your name?"

The pony turned round as far as he could, for unlike me he was tied up. "Merrylegs," he replied. "I carry the young ladies on my back. They are very fond of me."

He stopped and looked me up and down.

"Are you to live in the loose box?" he asked.

When I said I was, he sighed. "Well I hope you are good-tempered and don't bite."

Just then an ill-tempered-looking chestnut mare in the stall beyond said, "So it is for you that I was turned out of my box. What has the world come to when a fine lady like me loses her home to a colt like you?"

"I have turned no one out," I protested. "The man who bought me put me here, and, as for being a colt, I am four years old and a full-grown horse."

The chestnut horse said nothing but simply turned away.

Later, after the chestnut mare had been taken out, Merrylegs told me to pay no attention to what Ginger said. "She bites," he said. "One day she bit James Howard, our stableboy, and now the young ladies of the house are afraid to come in here on their own. I miss them," he added wistfully.

"Why should a horse bite anything but grass, hay and oats?" I said. "I don't, and I can't see why Ginger does."

"It's just a bad habit," Merrylegs said. "John Manley, our groom, does all he can to please her, and there couldn't be a kinder stableboy than James. So it's Ginger's own fault that she was turned out of her loose box and is now kept tethered."

The next day I was led into the yard by John Manley and given a good grooming. Just as I was being led back

into my box, my coat soft and bright, the squire came into the yard. "Take him out and give him a turn round the Highwood and back by the water-mill and the river," he said. "That'll show his paces."

I remembered my mother's words and my training and did my best to give John Manley a good ride. We started slowly, then we started trotting and cantering and when we were on the common by Highwood, he gave me the lightest touch of the whip and we had a splendid gallop.

"You'd like to follow the hounds, I think," he said when he pulled me up.

As we came into the park we met the squire and Mrs Gordon out walking.

"How does she go, John?" asked the squire.

"First rate, sir," answered John. "Fleet as a deer, and when we passed the men shooting rabbits, he didn't startle when the guns went off."

"Good, good," said the squire. "I'll take her out myself tomorrow."

We had a good ride, the squire and I, and when we came back, the mistress was waiting for us.

"Well my dear," she said. "How do you like him?"

"He's one of the most pleasant horses I've ever ridden," he said. "All we need now is a name for him."

"How about Ebony?" Mrs Gordon suggested. "Or Blackbird? After your uncle's old horse."

"He's far handsomer than Blackbird ever was," said the squire. "But he's black all right and he's beautiful."

"Then we should call him Black Beauty," said Mrs Gordon.

And that's how I got my name.

When James, the stable lad was told my name, he said to John Manley, "I'm surprised they didn't call him Rob Roy, for never were two horses more alike."

"Little wonder," said John. "For Farmer Grey's Duchess was the mother of them both."

So the poor horse that was killed in the hunt when I was young was my brother. No wonder my mother was so sad. It seems that horses have no family, at least not after they are sold.

CHAPTER FOUR
Ginger's Story

A few days later I had to go out with Ginger in the carriage. We worked well together, both doing our fair share and keeping in step so well that John never had to use the whip on either on us.

The next day, a Sunday it was, we were all turned out into the orchard.

There were five of us – me, Merrylegs, with whom I was now great friends, Ginger, who still seemed to resent the fact that I had been given the loose box, Justice, an old roan cob used for riding, and an old hunter, Sir Oliver, who was now retired but who was still a great favourite with the master.

What fun it was to run free and roll in the soft grass. Even Ginger was in a good mood and we fell into conversation.

"Where were you before you came here?" she asked.

When I told her all about my life at the farm and how kindly I had been broken, she shook her head sadly and said, "My life has been so different, for no one was ever kind to me."

As I listened to Ginger's story I began to think it no wonder that she was such a bad-tempered horse. She had been taken from her mother as soon as she could eat grass and turned into a field along with four or five other colts. "I didn't care for them," Ginger said, "And they didn't care for me."

"There was no kind master for us," she went on. "We weren't ill-used, but the man who looked after us gave us food and winter shelter, and that was all. He did little to stop local boys coming to our field and throwing stones at us. And that made us wild and made us think all boys were our enemies."

"What happened when you were broken in?" I asked.

"Three or four men came into the field one day and chased me into a corner. One of them caught me by the hair on my forehead. Another took hold of my nose and a third twisted my mouth open and forced a bit into it. I tried to rear up, the pain was so bad, but they held me where I was."

When I heard this, I remembered the gentle way that Farmer Grey had fitted my first bit into my mouth. "What happened next?" I asked.

"I was taken to a field where a man called Samson fitted a leading rein to my bridle and made me run round and round the field until I was exhausted. One day when I had been on the rein for hours, he put a saddle on me

and climbed on my back. I tried to buck him off, but he whipped me again and again."

I could hardly bear to listen, but there was no stopping Ginger now.

"Eventually I managed to throw him off. I galloped down the field and stood in the hot sun, too dazed to bother about the flies buzzing around the wounds that Samson's whip had inflicted on me.

"Later, Samson's father came into the field and gently led me to the stable. I snapped when I saw Samson standing by the door.

"'Idiot,' said the old man. 'That was a bad day's work. A bad- tempered man will never make a good-tempered horse.'"

I listened as Ginger went on to tell me how she had been sold to a London gentleman who knew nothing about horses and only wanted them to look fancy when they pulled his carriage.

"Fancy?"

"To ride with their heads held high all the time. And to make me do that, he had me fitted with a bearing rein which pulls your head back all the time."

"That must agonising," I said.

Ginger nodded. "One day I could stand it no more. The rein was so tight that my neck ached, my windpipe hurt and I could hardly breathe. I kicked and kicked as

hard as I could until I broke free. Of course, my master didn't want me after that and sold me."

"To a kinder man, I hope."

Ginger shook her head. "No, my next master told his groom to use the bearing rein, and the one after that, and the one after that."

"How many master have you had?" I asked.

"Far too many. I like it here, and I don't mean to be ill-tempered, but it's hard for me not to think of men as my enemies."

As the weeks went past, Ginger and I became good friends. She became happier and happier and her temper turned sweeter and sweeter.

"I do believe the mare is getting quite fond of me," said James one day.

"She'll soon be as good as Black Beauty," said John Manley. "Kindness is all she needed, poor thing."

CHAPTER FIVE
The Storm

And so I settled in at Birtwick. Ginger and I were used to pull the carriage, but as we both had racing blood in us and were both about fifteen-and-a-half hands high, we were just as good for riding as we were for driving.

I liked nothing better than the days when we all went out. The squire always took Ginger, and I always carried my mistress on my back. And with the young ladies on Merrylegs and Sir Oliver, we cantered across the fields having a fine time.

My mistress was a superb horsewoman: she was light and her touch was so gentle on the rein that I was guided almost without feeling it.

I had noticed that Sir Oliver's tail was very short, only six or seven inches long, but it was some time before I plucked up the courage to ask him if he had had an accident.

"Accident!" he snorted. "It was no accident. When I was young I was taken to a place where I was tied up so tight that I could hardly move and could do nothing to stop them cutting off my tail."

I was horrified. "Whatever did they do that for?" I asked. "It must have been agonising."

"For fashion," said Sir Oliver. "And it was sore, but it wasn't the pain that I really minded. That went away. It was not having anything to whisk away the flies that I really minded. Still do, but at least docking is no longer fashionable."

"It was for fashion that I was fitted with that dreadful bearing rein," said Ginger. "It was thought stylish to have a team with their heads held high on drives round the Park in London. And some people still fit them to their horses."

"Not so much around here any more," said Sir Oliver, "for when the master and mistress see a horse that isn't being given its head, they try to make the driver see how foolish and cruel bearing reins are."

That made me even prouder of the Gordons than I already was and when, a few days later, the master asked John to put me to the light cart as he had business in town I nuzzled up to him affectionately.

It had been raining heavily for several days and there was a brisk wind blowing. But we rode along at a good pace until we came to a small wooden bridge.

"I think we're in for a bad night," called the toll-keeper as we started to cross the bridge. "The river is rising fast."

When we got to the other side, the water was lying so

deep that it came up to my knees in places, but the master drove gently, so I was not too troubled and we soon reached the town.

I had to wait for quite a time for my master to finish his business, so it was quite late when we started out. The wind was blowing much harder by now, making the trees creak and sway as it howled around them. I trotted on through swirling leaves and deep puddles when suddenly there was a dreadful splitting sound and a mighty oak tree crashed into the road just in front of me.

John was down in a flash.

"What's to be done, John?" called the master.

"The tree has blocked the road, sir," John replied. "We'll have to go back to the crossroads and take the long road to the bridge. It'll add six miles to the journey."

And so, when we got to the bridge, the sun had set and it was almost dark. As soon as my feet were on the wood I knew something was wrong and stopped suddenly.

"Ride on, Beauty," said my master, giving me the lightest touch of the whip, but I refused to budge.

John got down from the cart and tried to lead me across the bridge but I dug my hooves in and refused to move.

"Come on, Beauty," John urged me. "What's the matter?"

How I wished I could speak and not just whinny, for then I could tell him that the bridge was unsafe.

John tugged at my bridle again, and just as he did so the toll-keeper ran out of his house on the other side of the river.

"Stay where you are," he shouted to make his voice heard. "The bridge is down in the middle. If you try to cross you'll fall in and drown, as like as not."

"Thank God for Beauty," cried my master.

John gently turned me into a road that ran by the river and eventually took us to the Park, where we found the gardener looking out for us.

"The mistress is in a dreadful state, sir," he said. "She's sent James out to search for you."

"When he comes back tell him I'm safe," said the master. "Walk on, Beauty."

Mrs Gordon must have heard us coming up the drive, for even before we came to a stop, she ran out of the front door towards us.

"Are you all right?" she cried. "You're so late I thought you must have had an accident."

"We may well have had if it hadn't been for Beauty," said the master, jumping down from the cart.

As he started to tell the mistress what had happened, John led me back to the stable where he gave me a special supper of good bran mash and some crushed beans, and made me a bed of straw that was so thick that I fell asleep almost as soon as I lay down on it.

CHAPTER SIX
Good News for James

One day when John and I were on our way home after having been out on the master's business, we saw a boy trying to jump a pony over a gate, but the pony refused and turned to one side.

I was horrified when the lad gave the pony a good whipping and then tried to make him take the gate again.

This time, the pony turned the other way and was again soundly whipped.

Just as we drew level, the little horse put his head down, threw up his back heels and sent the boy into a hedge.

"Serves him right," laughed John, watching the pony gallop off, the reins dangling around his head.

"I say," cried the boy. "Come and help me out!"

"I think you're in the right place," called John, "and that a few scratches will teach you not to leap a pony over a gate that's too high for him." And with that we rode off.

A few minutes later, as we passed a farmhouse, the farmer and his wife came running out and signalled us to stop. "Have you seen my boy?" asked the farmer. "He

went out an hour ago on my pony and it has just come back without him."

"Your pony's better off without a rider than the one we saw on him a few minutes ago."

"What do you mean, sir?" the farmer asked.

John told him what had happened. "I love horses," he said, "and it angers me to see them so badly treated."

"My poor Bill," cried the farmer's wife. "I must go and see if he's hurt."

"Get back into the house, woman," the farmer cried. "It's not the first time he's ill-used that horse, nor the second. It's time he learned a lesson."

That said, he turned to John and thanked him for leaving the boy where he was.

When we got back to the Birtwick Park, John told James what had happened.

"That must be Bill Bushby," said James. "Serve him right. I knew him at school and he was always putting on airs and graces just because he was a farmer's son. He used to bully the little 'uns until we put a stop to it, me and the other lads of his age.

"And he was cruel, too. Used to catch flies and pull their wings off. When he was caught, he was sat in a corner and not allowed out at playtime for a week."

John was leading me into my box by now and sent James to get me some oats.

Just then the master came into yard, clutching a letter.

"John," he said, a worried expression on his face. "Have you ever had any complaints to make of young James?"

"Why no, sir," said John. "He's honest, hard-working and respectful."

"And when he goes with the horses," continued the master, "have you ever known him stop to talk to his acquaintances, or go into houses where he has no business, leaving the horses outside?"

"Never, sir," said John. "And if anyone has been saying he has, or that James is in any way untrustworthy, let him face me and I'll soon put him right."

Neither of them had seen that James had come into the box and that he had heard most of what had been said. But sensing someone was there, the master turned round.

"James, my lad," he said with a smile in his voice. "Put these oats down and come here."

James did as he was bid.

"I'm glad that John has such a good opinion of you, for I have here a letter from my brother-in-law, Sir Clifford Williams. His old coachman is getting feeble and Sir Clifford wants me to find him a trustworthy young groom about twenty or twenty-one who knows his business."

James's eyes lit up when he heard that Sir Clifford would pay eighteen shillings a week at first while the old coachman trained him for the job, and that he would have a

stable suit, a driving suit, a bedroom of his own and a boy working for him.

"I don't want to part with you, and I know John Manley would miss you as sure as he would miss his right hand," said the squire.

"I wouldn't stand in the lad's way, sir," said John.

"How old are you, James?" asked the master.

"Eighteen, sir. Nineteen next May."

"That's young," said the squire. "What do you think, John."

"Why, sir, young James may be young, and although he hasn't had much driving experience yet, he was a firm, light hand and a quick eye, and no horses will be better looked after than any cared for by James Howard."

It was settled that James should go to Clifford Hall in about six weeks and in the meantime he was to get a much practice in driving the carriage as possible.

I never knew the carriage being taken out so often. We drove down country lanes and town streets, at first with John on the box alongside James, but soon with James on his own. But Ginger and I didn't mind. James had never been anything other than kind to us and we would do anything for him.

CHAPTER SEVEN
The Fire

It was during this time that the master and mistress decided to visit friends who lived forty-six miles from Birtwick Hall and that James was to drive them.

On the first day we drove thirty-two miles, up some fairly steep hills, but James encouraged us gently, kept our feet on the smoothest part of the road and twice asked the master if we could stop to rest, Ginger and I.

It was evening when we arrived at the hotel where we were to spend the night. James skilfully drove us under an arch into the stable yard where two ostlers came to unharness us. The head one was a pleasant, active little man with a crooked leg and a yellow-striped waistcoat.

He unharnessed me quickly, patting me gently as he did so, then led me into a stable with seven or eight stalls in it, horses in three of them. James stood by as we were rubbed down and cleaned.

The old man was very skilled and did the job so quickly that James could hardly believe it was done when the old man said it was. But when he inspected me, he found the job had been done perfectly.

"I thought I was quick," he said. "And John Manley quicker still, but you beat us both."

"Practice makes perfect," said the ostler. "And I've had forty years' practice."

After he had told James the story of his life, he asked about Ginger and me, "for better mannered, better kept horses it's hard to imagine. Who owns them?"

"Squire Gordon of Birtwick Park," said James.

"Ah, I've heard of him," said the ostler. "A fine judge of horses and one of the best riders in the country."

"True," said James, "but he doesn't ride as much now, not since his son was killed riding this beauty's brother."

And as the two men left the stable, my thoughts went back to that dreadful day when the hunt had galloped through the meadow where I had lived with my mother.

Just before we settled down for the night, another ostler led in a traveller's horse and while he was cleaning him a young man with a pipe in his mouth came in to gossip.

"Run up to the loft, Towler," said the ostler, "and put some hay down this horse's rack, will you? Only lay down your pipe."

A little later, James came in to see that we were settled for the night and then the door was locked.

I don't know how long I slept for, but when I woke the air was thick and choking and I could hear Ginger and the other horses coughing because of the smoke.

Suddenly someone shouted, "Fire!" and the old ostler ran into the stable. He got one horse out but when he tried to get to the one in the next stall, he was beaten back by the flames. Just then I heard James's quiet and cheerful voice saying, "Come, my beauties."

He had my bridle on quick as a flash and then he tied his scarf over my eyes and coaxed me out into the yard.

"Here!" he cried, untying the scarf. "Someone take this horse while I go and get the other."

I was so scared that when I saw James run back into the blazing stable I started to whinny. There was confusion all around. The horses clattered round the yard as the carriages in the coach house were rolled out lest they caught fire. Windows were being thrown open and people were shouting at the tops of their voices.

But I paid no attention. My eyes were fixed on the stable door where the smoke poured out thicker and thicker and I could see the flames lashing the stalls.

"James Howard! Are you there?" I heard the master call, his words almost drowned out by a loud crash from within the stable.

I started to fear the worst for James, but suddenly he came through the smoke, leading Ginger by the bridle. She told me afterwards that it was my whinnying that had given her the courage to come out. Had I not been making so much noise, she would have refused to come out and would probably have burned to death.

CHAPTER EIGHT
Going for the Doctor

The rest of the journey was very easy, and a little after sunset the next day we reached the house of my master's friend, where we spent a pleasant few days before returning home where James had much to relate to John Manley.

After he had told John about the fire he asked if there was any news about who was to replace him when he went to work for Sir Clifford.

"Little Joe Green at the lodge," said John

"But he's only fourteen-and-a-half," scoffed James, "and he's so small."

"But he's quick and willing and kind-hearted. And if, after six weeks, either of us decides it is not going to work out, then that will be that and the master will look for someone else."

The next day Joe came to the stables to learn all he could before James left. He was taught how to sweep out the stables, to bring in the straw and hay, to clean the harnesses and wash the carriage.

It was on Merrylegs that James let Joe practise brush-

ing and washing a horse, and my old friend complained to me that he didn't like being mauled about by a boy who knew nothing.

But after two weeks he told me that he thought the boy would work out very well. "He's a bright little fellow and always comes whistling to work," he said.

At last the day came when James was to go.

He was sad to leave his old friends, especially Merrylegs, but John cheered him up and after he had come to each of us in turn and given us a handful of oats, he was off.

Merrylegs missed him most of all. The old horse pined for several days and went off his food, but John Manley soon got his spirits up and within a few days he was his old self again.

* * *

It was a few days after James had left that I was awakened by the clanging of the stable bell. As I lay in the straw wondering what was happening, John Manley came running into my box. "Wake up, Beauty," he cried. "Tonight we must ride faster than we have ever ridden before, for the mistress's life depends on it."

He had the bridle on my head even as I was struggling to my feet, and as soon as I was standing the saddle was on my back.

We rode round to the Hall where the squire was waiting for us.

"Now, John," he said, thrusting a letter into the groom's hand. "There's not a moment to lose. Give this note to the doctor and ask him to get here as quickly as possible. Give Beauty a rest at the inn and be back as soon as you can."

It was a beautiful night. The moon hung high in the sky, making the frost that covered the countryside shine like the stars above. I galloped like the wind across fields, down country lanes and over rough farm tracks, needing neither whip nor spur to encourage me. If my mistress's life had depended on it, I would have galloped to the ends of the earth and back, let alone the eight miles from Birtwick Park to the doctor's house

My shoes clattered on the cobbles as we rode through the deserted streets and the clock was striking three as we stopped outside the doctor's door.

John rang the bell again and again, and when no one came, started to thump on it so hard that I was afraid he would break it down.

Suddenly an upstairs window flew open and Doctor White's head appeared.

"Who's that making such a commotion?" he cried, flicking the end of his nightcap from out of his eyes.

"John Manley, sir. Squire Gordon's groom," John called up. "The mistress is ill, and I have to give you this letter. Come quick or she will surely die."

The doctor was at the front door in no time, tucking his shirt into his trousers and struggling into his great coat. "My horse has been out all day," he said, "and is quite exhausted. My son has just been called out and has taken the other. I'll have to use yours."

John stroked my neck and must have felt how hot I was. "He came at a gallop all the way, sir," he said, "and I was to give him a rest, but I think the master would not be against it."

Then he noticed the whip in the doctor's hand. "You'll have no need of that, sir," he said. "Black Beauty will go till he drops."

The doctor climbed into the saddle and I could tell at once he was not a good rider, but I rode as fast as I could and was grateful when he pulled up at the bottom of a hill and told me to rest for a moment or two.

As soon as I had my breath back, we were off again and it wasn't too long before we reached the Park, where the master was waiting with Little Joe Green. The two men ran into the house and Joe led me back to the stables.

I had been riding so hard for so long that my legs were shaking and I could only stand and pant, sweat dripping off my soaking coat.

"Poor Beauty," Joe said as he rubbed me down. "Never mind, I'll take care of you."

The lad did his best, but because I was so hot he didn't give me a blanket as he should have done. But he did give me a pail of cold water which I drank thirstily, although I would rather have had the warm drink that John Manley would have given me.

When I had finished drinking, Joe gave me some hay and corn and, thinking he had done all the right things, left the stable and went to bed.

He hadn't been gone for long when I began to shiver. Oh, how I wished I had a warm blanket over me. I also wished that John Manley was by my side, but he was probably still walking the long walk back from the doctor's house.

After a long while, I heard John at the door. As soon as he saw me he gave a cry and ran to my side. "Stupid boy," he said through clenched teeth. "No blanket and no doubt the water in that bucket was cold when he gave it to you."

I was feeling very ill by now. I could hardly breathe and when I did my lungs felt as if they were on fire. John nursed me day and night, and was with me when the master came to see me.

"My poor Beauty," he said softly. "My good horse, you saved your mistress's life, Beauty. You saved her life."

I don't know how long I was ill for. I remember the horse doctor coming and bleeding me to lessen my fe-

ver, and after that I began to get better and I can clearly recall the night Joe Green's father came to see me.

"I wish you'd say a kind word to Joe," he said to John Manley. "The lad is heartbroken. He knows it was his fault, but it was only because he didn't know what to do."

I think that John must have done as he was asked, for by the time I was better, Joe Green was back at the stables. He became so attentive and careful that John began to trust him, although it was seldom that he was allowed to exercise either Ginger or me.

But one day when John was out with Justice in the luggage cart, the master wanted a note delivered to a friend three miles away. "You can take Black Beauty, he said. But ride carefully."

The job was soon done, but on the way back we saw a heavily laden cart, its wheels stuck in the stiff mud of some ruts. The driver was furiously whipping the horses.

"Stop that," cried Joe. "I'll help you lighten the load."

But the driver carried on regardless.

Joe urged me into a gallop and we headed for a house in the distance. When we got there, Joe told the man who answered his knock what he had seen, for it appeared that the man employed the carter.

"Thank you, my lad," said the man. "Will you give evidence before the magistrate?"

"That I will," Joe replied.

When we got back to the stable, Joe told John Manley what had happened.

"You did right, lad," said John. "Many folk would have ridden by and said 'twas none of their business."

I swear Joe grew an inch in height, so happy was he to have gained John Manley's approval, and as the months passed he became one of the finest stableboys who ever cared for me.

CHAPTER NINE
Goodbye to Birtwick Park

Sadly, Joe didn't look after us for long, for sad changes were about to descend on us.

We knew the mistress was often ill, for the doctor was called to the house more and more and as the months passed, the master smiled less and less.

Even so, none of us expected the news that fell upon us like a death knell one day. The mistress was so weak, we heard, that she had been ordered to go and live in a warm country for two or three years.

Miss Jessie and Flora, the Gordons' two children, were the first to go. They came into the yard to say goodbye to us all, and they hugged old Merrylegs over and over again.

My old friend was to be sold to the vicar, for his wife wanted a pony and Merrylegs was so gentle that he was the perfect horse for the job.

I heard the master tell John that Merrylegs had been sold on condition that he was never to be sold, and that when he became too old to work he was to be shot and buried rather than live a painful old age. I told Merrylegs

the first of what I had heard, but thought it best not to tell him the rest.

Joe Green had been hired to take care of Merrylegs and to help in the house.

John Manley had many offers of work and eventually decided that he would like to become a colt-breaker or horse-trainer. My master gave his faithful groom the name and address of his agent in London and promised that he would tell the man that he could recommend John Manley to anyone.

Ginger and I were to be sold to an old friend of the master's, an earl who lived in a fine estate called Earlshall Park.

Eventually the sad day came when the master and mistress were to leave. Ginger and I were harnessed to the carriage and taken to the Hall to carry the master and mistress to the railway station. Everyone else had gone, apart from Joe Green and John Manley and a few servants who brought out cushions and rugs when we came to a halt outside the front door. When they were all arranged, the master came down the steps, carrying the mistress. He placed her carefully in the carriage while the servants stood around crying.

"Goodbye," he said. "We shan't forget any of you." And then he got in the carriage and told John to drive on.

As we drove through the village, people came out of

their houses and I heard many of them say, "God bless them."

When we reached the station and the mistress bade John farewell, I felt the reins twitch, but John made no answer. Perhaps he was as moved as Joe Green was, for the lad had taken the luggage out of the carriage and was standing close by our heads to hide his tears.

The train puffed into the station and we watched the master carry the mistress on board. Then the door slammed shut and the train pulled away. We waited until all we could see was a trail of thin white smoke and then made our sad way back to the Hall for the last time.

The next morning Ginger and I were taken to Earlshall Park.

"There are no better horses in the world," John told the earl's coachman, Mr York. "But one thing I must tell you – we never used the bearing rein on either of them."

"Well, I'm afraid they must wear it here. I prefer the loose rein myself, and his lordship doesn't mind. But my lady insists on the latest style and the rein must be tight when she rides."

"I'm sorry to hear that," said John shaking his head.

It was time for him to go. He came round and patted and spoke to us for the last time, in a sad, sad voice. I held my face close to him, all I could do to say goodbye.

Then he was gone and I have never seen him since.

CHAPTER TEN
Earlshall Park

I now had a new home and a new master, and it wasn't long before I had a new name, too, for the earl decided to call me Baron.

The day after we arrived at Earlshall, Ginger and I were harnessed to the carriage by Robert the groom, and as the clock struck three, we were led round to the front of the house.

A few minutes later, I heard the rustle of silk and when I looked at the front door, I saw a grand lady come down the steps. She looked at us coldly but said nothing until she was in the carriage and told the coachman to walk on.

I had been fitted with a bearing rein for the first time in my life, because the countess was a woman of style and wanted her horses to hold their heads high. I did not mind it too much, for although I couldn't put my head down when I wanted to, the rein didn't pull my head any higher than I usually carried it.

But the next day, again at three o'clock, when the countess came down the steps to where we were waiting, she

called, "York, put these horses' heads higher. They are
not fit to be seen."

York did as he had been ordered, and I understood why
Ginger had hated the bearing rein when she had been
forced to wear it before Squire Gordon had bought her.
As we went up a steep hill, I found it almost impossible
to pull with my head forced back so high.

But the countess was still not satisfied, for the next day
she ordered that the rein be tightened even more. And
so, day by day, hole by hole, the bearing rein was short-
ened until it was so tight that, instead of looking forward
to having my harness being put on, I began instead to
dread it.

At last, I thought, after there had been no more short-
ening for several days, the worst was over, but I was wrong.

One day, after I had been at Earlshall for a week or
two, we were harnessed and taken to the front door at
three o'clock as usual. We waited and waited until eventually the countess came rustling down the steps, obviously agitated about something.

"York," she cried. "We can't go to the duchess's with
the horses looking like that. Are you never going to get
these horses' heads up? Raise them at once!"

York came to me first and pulled the rein so tight that
the bit cut into my mouth. Then he turned to Ginger.
Knowing what was coming, Ginger began to kick out

with all her strength. She was writhing so violently that suddenly she tripped over the carriage pole and tumbled to the ground, pulling me down with her.

York sat on her head to stop her struggling while I was set free and taken to my stable. I was so angry and sore that for the first time in my life I would have kicked the first person to come near me.

Before long, Ginger was led in by York.

"Confound these bearing reins," York said as he let down my head. "I knew we would have some mischief soon. The master will be furious, and I am sure to get the blame for the countess being late for the duchess's garden party."

The earl was angry and when he came into the stable yard I heard him tell York he shouldn't have given way to the countess about using bearing reins.

"In that case, sir," said York, "I would prefer only to take my orders from you."

But it didn't make much difference. The next time I was harnessed for the carriage, I had the bearing rein.

Ginger was luckier. She was never put into the carriage again. She was given to the earl's son as a hunter. In her place at the carriage pole was a horse called Max, who was obviously used to that dreadful rein for he didn't seem to complain about it.

"How do you bear it?" I asked him one day.

"Because I must," he replied. "Even though it is short-ening my life, and will shorten yours, too."

For four miserable months, I suffered the rein. I had never foamed at the mouth before, but now the action of the sharp bit on my tongue and jaw made me froth. Some people think that it is very fine to see this. "What hand-some creatures," they say when they see a team drive past, heads held high, foaming at the mouth. But it is as unnatural for a horse as it would be for a man.

Besides that, there was the constant pressure on my windpipe and when I returned from work, my neck and chest were strained, my mouth and tongue tender, and I felt worn and depressed.

In my old home, John and the others had been my friends. At Earlshall, I had none.

* * *

In the spring, York drove the earl and the countess to London, and while they were away, I was used for riding by one of their daughters, Lady Anne. She was a fine horsewoman who rode side-saddle, as did all the lady riders.

We often went out, sometimes accompanied by a man called Blantyre who rode a mare named Lizzie.

Blantyre often sang Lizzie's praises. "She's a wonder," he would say. "Superb to ride and so full of life."

One day, when Blantyre and Lady Anne came into the

stables, I heard her tell the lad to put the side-saddle on Lizzie and the other one on me.

"What are you doing?" asked Blantyre.

"I plan to ride this Lizzie that you praise so much," Lady Anne replied, "to see if she is as good as you say she is."

Blantyre tried to make her change her mind. "Please don't," he said. "She's far too nervous for a lady."

"Don't be silly," said Lady Anne. "Now help me up."

Blantyre could see that it was useless to argue, so he helped Lady Anne into the saddle and we set off towards the village where Blantyre had a letter to deliver.

"I won't be longer than five minutes," he said when he dismounted outside a house and hung my reins over the gate.

"Don't hurry," said Lady Anne. "Lizzie and I won't run away."

A few moments after Blantyre had gone into the house, a boy came down the road with a group of colts, whipping them on. One of them strayed too close to Lizzie, who was obviously frightened. I tried to calm her down, but she was having none of it.

Seconds later she was off, galloping down the street and out of the village.

I whinnied as loudly as I could, and Blantyre came running out of the house.

Seeing Lady Anne in the distance, he jumped into the saddle and we took off after her.

The road ran straight for a mile and a half and then divided. Lady Anne was so far away by this time that we had lost sight of her.

"Which way did the lady on the bay mare go?" Blantyre shouted at a boy standing at the fork.

"To the right, sir. Into the park."

We galloped across the park, which was rough and uneven and full of potholes, and were gradually closing the distance between ourselves and Lady Anne when we saw Lizzie race up to a stream that flowed across the park, sheltered by a steep bank beyond.

She leapt over the water but her front hooves caught the top of the bank and she went crashing down, throwing her rider to the ground.

"Come on, Baron," cried Blantyre. "You can do it."

With one mighty leap I cleared the stream and the bank, and no sooner were my feet on the ground than Blantyre had pulled on the reins and brought me to a stop.

He jumped down and ran to where Lady Anne was lying. Very gently he raised her head so that I could see her face was deathly pale. "Dear Anne," he said softly, "do say something."

My mistress moaned softly, and Blantyre laid her head back on the ground. "You there," he shouted to some

men who had been cutting plants nearby. "One of you take that horse and ride to the doctor's then onto the Hall and tell them to send a carriage as quickly as they can."

The man who climbed into my saddle was no horseman, but we made it, and Lady Anne was brought home later that afternoon.

There was a great deal of excitement when I was taken into the stable where, two days later, Blantyre came to see me. "There she is, the horse that saved my Anne," he said to the groom and stroking my forehead gently. "She'll be riding again soon, and please, I beg of you, make sure that from now on she only goes out on Baron."

CHAPTER ELEVEN
I Move on Again

The earl and countess stayed in London for several weeks, and during that time one of the men looking after us was a man called Reuben Smith. Smith was clever and gentle, and everyone liked him, but he had one bad habit, he drank.

York had done his best to conceal Reuben's drinking from the master and mistress, but one night he had had to drive a party home from a ball and had been so drunk that he couldn't hold the reins and one of the gentlemen in the party had had to mount the box and drive the ladies home.

Reuben had been dismissed, of course, and his wife and children had had to leave the pretty cottage they had lived in by the main gate.

I learned all this from Max, for it had happened some time before Ginger and I arrived at Earlshall, for by the time we got there, Smith had been taken back on again after he had promised faithfully that he would never drink again.

One day, not long after Lady Anne had had her fall,

Reuben took me to town on an errand and left me at the White Lion's stables.

"Feed him and have him ready for me at four," he said.

He didn't come back till five and when he did, he told the lad that he had met with some friends and that he'd be back at six.

"There's a loose nail in one of your horse's shoes," said the lad. "Shall I fix it for you."

"Don't bother," slurred Smith. "I'll take care of it when we get home."

It was nine o'clock before he came for me, and when he did he was well and truly drunk.

"Have a care, Mr Smith," the landlord called, seeing the unsteady way in which Reuben climbed into the saddle.

Reuben answered him angrily and dug his heels into my sides to urge me on. We were cantering while we were still in the High Street, and by the time we were out of town, I was being whipped into a gallop.

The roads were stony, and it wasn't long before my shoe became looser and then came off altogether. If Smith hadn't been so drunk he would have noticed something was wrong, but all he did was curse me and whip me to go even faster than I already was.

My foot was hurting terribly, the hoof was split and I could feel that the inside was badly cut. I was in agony

when I suddenly stumbled and fell violently onto my knees. Smith flew over my shoulders and landed with a loud crash some distance in front of me.

I got to my feet and limped to the side of the road. Smith made a slight effort to rise, then groaned and slumped back to the ground and lay there quite motionless.

It was midnight before anyone came to look for us.

"Look, there's Baron," said a voice I recognised. It was Robert, the groom.

He came up to me and knelt down, taking my injured foot in his hands.

"He's bad in the foot," he said tenderly. "His hoof is cut to pieces and his knees are about as bad."

Meanwhile, someone else had found Reuben. "I'm afraid he's dead," he said.

"He must have been drunk, Ned" said Robert. "No one in his right mind would ride a horse with a shoe missing over ground like this."

I watched as they loaded Reuben's body onto a cart and then Robert very gently bound my foot with his handkerchief and slowly led me the three miles home.

When I was safely in my stall, he gave me some corn then tied wet cloths round my torn knees. Next he bound my foot in a poultice to clean it and draw out the heat before the horse doctor came in the morning.

When he came, I was carefully examined. "He should be all right," he said, "but he'll never lose the scars that will be left on his knees."

I slowly got better, and when I was able to walk I was turned out in a field to run free until I was completely recovered. At first I was on my own and felt lonely, but one day I was overjoyed to see my old friend Ginger being let loose in the field.

My joy was short-lived for she told me that Lord George, the earl's son, had hunted her to the very limits of her endurance and she was now no longer up to the job. "And so," she said, "here we are, both of us ruined in our prime of youth and strength – you by a drunkard and I by a fool."

Not long afterwards the earl and countess returned from London. The earl was furious when he heard what had happened to us.

"Three hundred pounds flung away for no earthly reason," he thundered at York. "But what I care about more is that my old friend, Squire Gordon, thought his horses would be well cared for here."

He looked at Ginger. "We'll keep the mare for twelve months and see if we can bring her back to form, but the black one must be sold. I could not have knees like that in my stables."

"I know a man in Bath," said York. "He often wants

horses at a good price, and I know he looks after them well."

"Write to him," said the earl. "As long as he's well looked after, I don't mind how much he fetches."

About a week later Robert came into the field and slipped a halter on my neck. I didn't have time to nuzzle up to Ginger, but we neighed to each other as I was led off, and she trotted along by the hedge, anxiously calling to me as long as she could hear the sound of my feet.

CHAPTER TWELVE
A Job Horse and its Drivers

I was bought by the master of a stables where horses and carriages are kept to be rented out to whoever has the money to pay for them. I had to go by train, which was hard at first, but I soon got used to the puffing, rushing and whistling, and when I reached the end of my journey I was put in a comfortable stable and was well looked after.

The only thing that troubled me was that the stalls were laid out on a slope, and as my head was kept tied to the manger I was always on the slope, which I found very tiring.

My new master kept a good many horses. Sometimes he drove them, and sometimes the horse and chaise were let out to gentlemen or ladies who drove themselves.

None of these was as good or as gentle as John Manley or Mr York. Some I called tight-rein drivers, who never let the reins go slack and talked about "keeping the horses well in". Others were loose-rein drivers. They paid little attention to their horses as they drove along, gossiping about this and that, or pointing out the sights. They let

the reins drop so loose that it was difficult not to stumble and go sideways, but they didn't seem to notice.

Then there was the steam-engine kind of driver, who wanted us to start at full speed and shouted angrily if the pace was slackened for as much as a moment. And when they stopped, they hauled in the reins so suddenly that I skidded to an abrupt halt.

But there were good drivers, too. Kind men who knew about horses and how to drive them. One of these good souls was a man called Mr Barry who took such a liking to me that, when his doctor advised him to take more exercise, he persuaded my master to sell me to him so that he could ride me as often as he wanted.

Mr Barry was an unmarried gentleman who lived in lodgings in Bath. With no stable of his own, he hired one for me near to his rooms, and took on a man called Filcher. When I heard Mr Barry order that I should have the best hay with plenty of oats, crushed beans and bran, I thought I was going to be well off.

For a few days all went well. Filcher kept the stable light and airy and groomed me thoroughly, but after a while I noticed I was getting less and less oats. I had the beans but found them mixed more and more with bran rather than oats, and in two or three weeks this began to show in my condition.

One day, when I was not in the best of spirits, Mr Barry

rode me out into the country to visit a farmer, a friend of his.

"Your horse doesn't look nearly as well as he did when you first had him," said the farmer.

Mr Barry agreed. "But," he added, "my groom tells me that horses are always dull in the autumn."

"Fiddlesticks," cried the farmer. "'Tis only August in any case. This horse is not being fed properly. You'd best check into your stable, for there are men bad enough to rob a horse of its food."

Could I but speak, I would have told Mr Barry that the farmer was right, for every morning Filcher brought his small son into the stable and gave him a basket full of my oats.

My master must have checked, for a few days later just as the boy was leaving the stable, two policemen arrived.

"We know your father keeps rabbits," I heard them say to the lad. "Show us the place where he keeps his rabbit food."

Filcher was in my stall at the time and before he could do anything about it, his son had led the policemen to the oat bin. "In there," he said.

They found my groom where he was, and although he denied that he had been stealing my oats, the policemen had found the evidence of an empty bag like that which was found full of oats in the boy's basket.

The man and boy were led away to be locked up. I heard afterwards that the boy was not held to be guilty, but the man was sentenced to prison for two months.

* * *

My new groom arrived a few days later. Alfred Smirk was his name, and never was a man more suitably named. He was a tall, good-looking man who spent a great deal of time fixing his hair, brushing his whiskers and sorting his necktie.

And every time my master said anything to him, Smirk would say, "Yes, sir! Yes, sir," as if my master was the most important man in the world.

Everyone thought that my master was lucky to have got Smirk, but he was a fake – the laziest groom I have ever met. He never cleaned my feet or checked my shoes. He hardly brushed me and never cleaned my loose box properly, only taking a little of the dirty straw away before covering what was left with clean. The smell became so bad that my eyes began to smart and became inflamed and my appetite was not half of what it should have been.

One day when Mr Barry came into the stable, he noticed how foul the smell was. "Should you not give that stall a good scrub and throw down plenty of water?" he asked.

"Yes, sir! Yes, sir!" said Alfred Smirk, "but it is danger-

ous to throw down water in a horse's box, for they are
apt to take cold, sir."

"Could it be the drain?" asked my master.

"Well, sir, now you mention it, I think the drain does
sometimes send back a smell."

"Then send for a bricklayer and have it seen to," ordered Mr Barry.

The builder came and could find nothing wrong, but
charged my master five shillings all the same and my
stable still smelt as bad as before.

My feet became so sore from standing on moist straw
that when my master took me out I found it difficult to
keep my footing.

When he mentioned this to Smirk, the groom said, "Yes,
sir! Yes, sir! I have noticed this myself when I exercise
the horse."

Now Smirk hardly exercised me at all, but he fed me as
if he did and I became heavy and dull and sometimes
restless and feverish. But he was so ignorant he did not
know that a meal of green meal or bran mash would
have cooled me down, and poured all sorts of medicines
down my throat, which made me feel and uncomfortable.

One day my feet were so tender and I was feeling so
out of sorts, I stumbled when trotting with the master on
my back. He led me to the blacksmith.

The man looked at my feet one by one and said, "Your horse has got the thrush. I wonder your groom has not seen to it."

My master asked how I could have caught such a thing.

"From standing in foul stables where the straw is never properly cleared. Send your man round with the horse tomorrow. I will tend to hoof and tell your man how to apply the liniment I will give him."

The next day I had my feet cleaned and soaked in strong lotion, and very unpleasant it was too.

He told Mr Barry to make sure that all the litter was taken out of my stall every day and the floor washed and dried before fresh straw was put down. I was to have bran mash and a little green meal and not so much corn until my feet were well again.

I soon regained my health, but Mr Barry was so disgusted by being deceived by two grooms – first Filcher and now Smirk – that he decided to give up keeping a horse and to hire one when he wanted to go out riding.

So I was kept till my feet were quite sound, and then sold again.

CHAPTER THIRTEEN
A London Cab Horse

No doubt a horse fair is a very amusing place to those who have nothing to lose. But to a horse, whose future is at stake, it is a very different matter.

Many people came to see me. They prodded me, felt me over, looked in my mouth. But those who were gentlemen always turned away when they saw my knees, saying that they couldn't have a horse with such blemishes in their stables.

One man stopped and poked me here and poked me there so roughly that when he made an offer of twenty-three pounds for me, I was afraid I may be sold to him. But I was relieved when Mr Barry's agent said that was not enough.

A short while afterwards, a man with kind grey eyes looked me up and down and examined me very carefully. When he spoke to me, his voice was soft and gentle and I knew I could be happy with him.

"Easy does it, old fellow," he said tenderly, then turned to the agent and offered twenty-four pounds for me.

"Twenty-five and he's yours," came the reply.

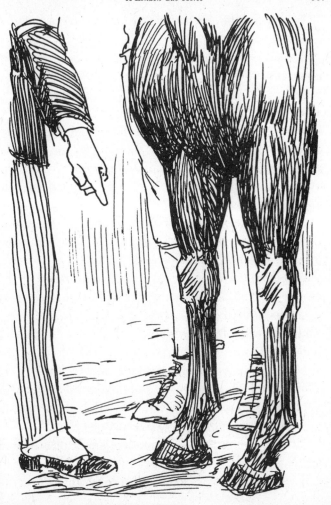

"Twenty-four pounds and ten shillings, and not a penny more," said the man.

"Done!" said the dealer. "And you may depend upon it that's cheap for such a horse. And if you want him for cab work, he's a bargain."

The money was paid, and I was led to an inn where my new master had a saddle and bridle waiting for me. He gave me a good feed of oats, standing by me as I ate, talking gently to me, and half-an-hour after I had finished he climbed into the saddle and we were on our way to London.

We rode through pleasant country lanes and roads until we came to the great London Road which took us into the city. The gas lamps were already lit and I could see streets to the left of me and streets to the right, streets crossing each other: so many streets I thought we would never come to the end of them.

But after we had passed a line of cabs and my master had hailed some of the drivers, we turned into a narrow street and stopped outside a slightly shabby house.

My master whistled loudly and the door flew open. A young woman ran out, followed by a girl and a boy.

"Open the gates, Harry, and bring a lantern."

The next minute they were standing round me in a small stable yard.

"Is he gentle, Father?" the little girl asked.

"Yes, Dolly. As gentle as a kitten. Come and pat him."

"Let me give him a bran mash while you rub him down," said the children's mother.

"Do, Polly, for it's just what he wants."

Later, after I had been well fed, I laid down in my new stall. It was warm and clean and the straw was as fresh as spring. I knew I was going to be happy.

* * *

My new owner was called Jeremiah Baker but as everyone called him Jerry I shall do the same. Polly, his wife, was plump, trim and tidy with smooth dark hair, dark eyes and a merry mouth. Harry was twelve, a tall, good, well-tempered lad. His sister was four years younger and just like her mother. I have never known such a happy family.

Jerry had his own cab and another horse, called Captain, who worked in the cab all morning, while I went out in the afternoon. Jerry was a gentle as John Manley and never once used the bearing rein, although when we went into fashionable parts of town, I was sorry to see teams of horses pulling fine carriages, their heads held far too high.

On the first day, Harry helped Jerry to groom me, and Polly and Dolly gave me a slice of apple and a piece of bread and were so kind they made me feel as if I had been the Black Beauty I once had been.

My first week as a cab horse was hard as I was not used to the noise and crowds of London. But Jerry was a good driver and we made a fine team.

He never worked on Sundays, even though he could have charged extra money, for he said that Sunday was a day of rest for all God's creatures. Nor would he drive me fast, even if he was offered.

I remember one day when two wild-looking young men hailed our cab.

"Victoria Station," one of them said. "Quick as you can for we must catch a train at one o'clock. There's an extra shilling in it for you."

"I will take you, sirs, for the regular fare, but I won't overtire my horse."

"Take my cab, sirs," said one of the other drivers. "Jerry won't go faster than a slow trot."

The two men got into the other cab and the driver whipped his horse to drive off as fast as it could.

Jerry stroked my nose and said, "No, old boy, a shilling would not pay for that sort of thing. Nothing would."

CHAPTER FOURTEEN
An Old War Horse

I got to know Captain very well, and one day he told me
that he had been broken in and trained as an army horse.
He had enjoyed trotting with the other horses, turning
together to the right and left, halting when the command
was given, and dashing forward to the sound of a trum-
pet or the signal of an officer.

"One of the worst parts was when we were put aboard
a great ship to be taken to the Crimea, where the British
and French were at war with the Russians. We could not
walk off the land onto the ship, so they put great straps
under our bodies and we were swung over the water on
to the deck."

"What was it like?" I asked.

"Dreadful. We were put in small stalls and for the en-
tire voyage never saw the sky and we were never exercised. When the wind blew, the ship rolled around and
we were badly knocked about. But at last it came to end
and after we were swung over the water again, we found
ourselves on land again and we snorted and neighed for
joy."

"Did you see any fighting?" I wanted to know.

"Often!" he said. "Sometimes we had to stand around for hours waiting for the word of command, and then we sprang forward as eagerly as if there were no cannon balls, bayonets or bullets to be fired, for as long as we felt our rider firm in the saddle and his hand steady on the bridle we weren't scared, even when bombshells whirled through the air and burst into thousands of pieces.

"My master and I came through many actions without a wound," Captain went on. "I saw horses shot down with bullets, pierced through with lances and gashed with fearful sabre cuts. I saw brave men cut down and I heard the cries and groans of the dying. But my master's cheery voice made me feel as if I could not be killed."

"He must have been a good horseman," I said.

Captain nodded. "He cantered me over ground slippery with blood and frequently had to turn me to avoid trampling on a wounded man or horse. But I never felt terror until one dreadful day."

"What happened?" I asked.

"It was early one autumn morning. As usual we'd been up an hour before daybreak ready for the day's work. There was a sense of excitement in the air, and when we heard the sound of enemy gunfire, one of the officers rode up and ordered the men to mount.

"We were at the head of the line, and as we waited for

the command to move forward, my master patted me on the neck and said, 'We shall have a day of it today, but we'll do our duty as we have done.'

"I cannot tell all that happened that day. We were given the command to charge several times, and by the time we made the last one we were well used to the roar of the guns and the rattle of musket fire.

"We regrouped to make our final charge across a valley right in front of the enemy's cannon. From the right and left and from the front, shot and shells poured down on us. Many a brave man went down. Many a horse fell and went without a rider and ran wildly out of line. But then, terrified of being alone, galloped back to be among his old companions."

"No one stopped, no one turned back. Our ranks thinned as our comrades fell, but we closed in to keep together and galloped faster and faster towards the cannon, all clouded with smoke with red fire flashing through it."

Captain stopped for a moment as if the memory was too painful, but then he went on.

"My dear master was cheering on his comrades, his right arm raised on high, when a cannon ball whizzed past my head and struck him. I felt him stagger with shock and the reins went loose as he fell from the saddle.

"I wanted to stay with him and not leave him under

the rush of horse's hooves. But it was useless. I began to tremble, as I have never trembled before, and just then another soldier whose horse had been shot from under him, jumped up into my saddle and urged me forward.

"But we were soon forced back, though some of the horses were so badly wounded that they could scarcely move for loss of blood. Others were struggling to rise to their feet, their hind legs shattered by shot. Their groans were piteous to hear, and the look on their faces as we rode past will stay with me forever."

"What happened to them?" I asked.

"After the battle the wounded soldiers were brought in and the dead were buried. The badly wounded horses were all shot. The ones that had only slight wounds were brought back and cared for, but even so for every four horses that went out that morning, only one returned in the evening.

"I never loved any master as much as the one killed that day. I went into many more battles and was only wounded once, but not seriously. And when the war was over, I came back to England as sound and strong as when I went out."

"Do you know why they were fighting?" I asked.

"No! That's more than a horse can understand, but the enemy must have been very wicked if it was right to go all that way overseas on purpose to kill them."

CHAPTER FIFTEEN
London Life

I remember the day we were waiting at the cab stand when a young man carrying a heavy bag slipped on a piece of orange peel lying on the pavement and fell down heavily.

Jerry, who had been waiting for a fare, jumped down to help the man to his feet and into a nearby shop. Ten minutes later, the man came out and asked Jerry to take him to the South-Eastern Railway. "That fall has made me late and I have to catch the twelve o'clock train."

"I'll do my best to get you there," said Jerry, "if you think you are well enough to travel."

"I must get that train," said the young man, who looked dreadfully white and ill. "I'll pay an extra fare."

Jerry helped the man into the cab then jumped up on the box and said, as he twitched the reins, "Now then, Jack, my boy. Spin along. We'll show them how we can get over the ground."

It is always difficult to drive fast in the city in the middle of the day when the streets are full of traffic, but Jerry and I were used to it and no one could beat us at getting

through when we were set upon it. I was quick and bold and trusted Jerry without question.

The streets were especially busy that day, but we got on pretty well until we got to Cheapside where the traffic was jammed.

"I think I'd better walk," called the young man. "I shall never get there if this goes on."

"I'll do all that can be done, sir," said Jerry. "This block-up cannot last much longer and your luggage is very heavy for you to carry."

Just then the cart in front started to move and we had a good run all the way to London Bridge, where we trotted along with lots of other cabs and carriages and whirled into the station at eight minutes to the hour.

"You have saved me more money than I can ever pay for," said our thankful passenger. "Take this extra half-crown."

"No, sir," said Jerry. "Thank you all the same."

He called a porter and told him to take the young man's luggage to the Dover Line, then drove off before the man could force the half-crown on him.

When we got back to the cab stand, the other drivers began to tease Jerry about the extra fare they had heard him being offered.

"He's a humbug," said one of them. "Remember the day he wouldn't take the two young men from outside

the inn, even although they offered him an extra shilling."

"Look here, lads," cried Jerry. "The gentleman offered me half-a-crown, but I didn't take it. 'Twas quite enough for me to see how glad he was to catch his train. And if Jack and I choose to have a quick run now and then to please ourselves, then that's our business and none of yours."

* * *

One day as Jerry was putting me into the shaft, a gentleman walked into the yard.

"Your servant, sir," said Jerry.

"Good morning, Mr Barker," said the gentleman. "I should be glad to make some arrangements with you for taking Mrs Briggs regularly to church on Sunday mornings. We go to New Church now, and it is rather farther than she can walk comfortably."

"Sorry, sir," said Jerry. "I only have a six-day licence."

"But you could easily alter it. I would see you did not lose by it, and I know Mrs Briggs would rather be driven by you than anyone else."

"I should be glad to oblige the lady, sir," said Jerry, "but I had a seven-day licence once and it was too hard on me and the horses. Year in and year out, and never a day's rest, never a Sunday with my wife and children, and never able to go to church."

Mr Briggs tried and tried to persuade Jerry to change his mind, but it was no good.

"Very well," said the gentleman. "Don't trouble yourself, Mr Barker. I will inquire elsewhere."

And with that, he turned round and walked away.

When Polly came into the yard, Jerry told her what had happened.

"Mrs Briggs is a good customer," he said. "I often take her shopping or on her calls, and she always pays me fair and honourable like the lady she is. No beating down, or saying she's only had me for two-and-a-half hours and not three as some folks do. And if I don't oblige her on this matter, it is likely we shall lose the Briggs altogether."

"Jerry Barker," said Polly. "Even if you were paid a sovereign for taking them to church, I would not have you a seven days' cabman again. I'd rather go without than have you working on Sundays."

News that Jerry had lost one of his best customers soon spread among the other cabmen. Some of them thought he was a fool, but two or three stuck up for him and there was a long argument one afternoon.

"There shouldn't be no need for cabs on Sundays," said Jerry after everyone had had their say. "A good man will find a way to get about without one on a Sunday. If his church is too far for him to walk to, then let him choose to worship in another closer to his home. And if it is

raining, then let him wear a mackintosh to walk to church. If a thing is right it can be done, and if it is wrong it can be done without."

And none of the other cabmen had any answer to that.

* * *

Two or three weeks after this, Jerry and I came home one night to find Polly waiting for us, obviously bursting to tell us some news.

"You'll never guess, Jerry," she said, "but Mrs Briggs sent a servant this afternoon to ask you to pick her up at eleven tomorrow. And when I told the girl that we supposed the Briggs had employed someone else by now, she told me that her master had been really angry with you for refusing to take Mrs Briggs to church on Sunday, but that none of the other drivers they have tried are as good as you, Jerry. Some are too fast, and some too slow. And others have cabs that are not nearly as clean as yours, and nothing will suit her but to use you again."

"Hear that, Jack?" said Jerry, stroking my forehead. "We're to carry the gentry again."

After this, Mrs Briggs wanted Jerry as often as before but never on a Sunday, although we did work one Sabbath.

It happened after we had come home very late one Saturday night, both of us looking forward to our day of rest.

In the morning when Jerry was cleaning me in the yard, Polly came out of the house.

"What is it, my dear?" asked Jerry.

Poor Dinah Brown has just had a letter to say that her mother is dangerously ill, and Dinah must go to her right away if she wishes to see her alive. But the old lady lives more than ten miles away, and if Dinah takes a train to the nearest station, she has a four-mile walk."

Jerry said nothing.

"She wants to know if you'll take her in the cab," said Polly. "And she promises faithfully to pay you as soon as she has the money."

"It's not the money," said Jerry. "I don't want to lose my Sunday. I'm tired and the horses are tired, too."

"You know we should do unto others as we would have them do unto us," said Polly, "and though it won't be the same without you, I know that if it was my mother who was dying, I would beg you to take me to her in the cab."

"Why, Polly," laughed Jerry, "you're as good as a minister, and as I've had my Sunday sermon already, tell Dinah I'll be round to get her at ten o'clock. And on the way back, call on Mr Braydon, the butcher, and ask him if he will lend me his trap, for I know he never uses it on a Sunday, and I'm sure Jack would like a change."

Mr Braydon's trap was a light, high-wheeled gig that felt like pulling nothing, after a week at the cab.

It was a fine May day, and we were soon out of town. It was lovely once more to have the sweet smells of the country in my nostrils, and the soft country roads were a treat to trot on.

When we arrived at Dinah's mother's farmhouse, I was turned out into a meadow where I grazed the sweet grass, rolled over and over, frolicked happily, then lay down and dozed in the warm sunshine. It was the first time I had been in a field since I had left poor Ginger at Earlshall.

When we got home, Polly and Dolly were in the yard. Jerry gave his little girl a bunch of wild flowers and hawthorn he had picked for her and bound with long sprays of ivy. She clapped her hands in delight when she saw it, and Polly smiled gently when Jerry said to her, "Well, Polly, I have not lost my Sunday after all, for the birds were singing hymns in every bush and I joined in the service. And as for Jack, he was as sprightly as a young colt less than half his age."

* * *

On cold winter days, Dolly would often run to the corner to see if Jerry and I were at the cab rank waiting for a fare, and if we were she would come back a few minutes later with some hot soup or pudding that Polly had cooked.

One day, when she had brought her father a basin of

soup and was standing by his side as he ate it, a gentleman hailed him with his raised umbrella. Jerry gave the
bowl to Dolly and was about to take my cloth off, when
the man cried, "No, no! Finish your soup, my friend. I
have not much time, but I can wait till you have done
and seen your little girl safely on her way."

"There, Dolly," said Jerry. "There's a real gentleman
for you."

When Jerry had finished his soup and taken Dolly across
the road, the gentleman asked to be taken to Clapham
Rise, and when we got to his house the front door flew
open and three dogs bounded down the path to greet
their master. After he had paid Jerry, he came round and
patted me, which was a rare thing for a gentleman to do.
Ladies used to pat me now and then, but ninety-nine
out of one hundred gentlemen would as soon think of
patting a steam engine that drew a train than they would
of patting a cab horse.

We often carried the gentleman after that, and one day
he and another man asked us to take them to Rye Street.
When we got there, the gentleman's friend went into a
shop and while we were waiting for him, we noticed a
cart with two fine horses harnessed to it standing outside a wine shop. There was no one with them, and I
never did find out how long they had been standing there,
but they must have decided that they had waited long

enough for after a minute or two, they began to move off.

They hadn't gone far when the carter came out of the shop and ran after them. When he caught them, he took his whip and began lashing the two horses angrily. When our gentleman saw what was happening, he ran to the carter and cried, "If you don't stop that, I will have you taken to the magistrate for leaving your horses unattended and for brutal conduct."

The carter had obviously been drinking, for his words were slurred as he cursed our gentleman loudly before clambering onto the cart and taking the reins.

The gentleman took a notebook out of his pocket and, looking at the name and address on the side of the cart, wrote something down.

"What do you want with that?" growled the driver.

But the gentleman simply nodded and smiled grimly.

By this time, his friend had finished his business and was back in the cab. "I would have thought, Wright," he said to our gentleman as he climbed in, "that you had enough to do already without troubling yourself with other people's horses and servants."

"Do you know why the world is such a bad place?" said Mr Wright after a few moments, and when his friend made no reply he went on, "It's because people only think about their own business and won't trouble themselves

to stand up for others. And if you think I'm an interfering old busybody, then I'll tell you that many a master has thanked me for letting him know how badly his horses have been used."

And as we trotted to Clapham Rise I heard Jerry say to himself, "I knew I wasn't wrong when I told Dolly that Mr Wright is a real gentleman."

* * *

One day when we were at the cab stand waiting for a fare, a shabby cab drawn by a tired old chestnut mare drew up beside ours. Her bones were plainly showing through her dull, ill-kept coat. Her knees were in poor condition and her forelegs looked unsteady.

I had been eating hay and the wind rolled some of it in her direction. I tried not to look as the poor creature strained her long neck to get to it then turned round to see if there was any more. There was a hopeless look in her eyes, but there was something about her that made me think I had seen her before.

Suddenly she caught my eye and said, "Black Beauty! Is that you?"

It was Ginger, but how changed she was. Her fetlocks and legs were swollen, her face once so full of spirit and life was now a picture of suffering, and I could tell by the way her sides heaved when she breathed and by her bad cough that she was in poor health.

Our drivers were standing together a little way off, so I sidled up to my old friend so we could talk. It was a sad tale she had to tell.

She had been rested for a year at Earlshall Park then sold to a gentlemen who looked after her well at first. But one day he rode her so long and hard that the old back strain she had developed when she had been a hunter returned.

She was sold right away, but her next owner didn't keep her for long, and so she was sold again and again until she was bought by a man who owned several cabs and horses which he rented to other drivers.

"The man who hires me now pays a great deal of money to the owner, so I work every day – Sundays too."

"You used to stand up for yourself when you were ill-treated," I said.

"I did it once," Ginger sighed, "but it's no use. Men are our masters, and if they are cruel and have no feelings, there is nothing a horse can do. You look well off, and I'm happy for you, but I wish I was dead. And I hope to die at my work and not be sent to the knacker's yard to be slaughtered."

I was so sad that I put my nose to hers but could think of nothing to say to make her feel better. And just as her owner came towards us, she said, "You are the only friend I ever had."

Her driver tugged at her mouthpiece and backed her out of the line.

A few days later a cart carrying a dead horse passed the cab stand. Its head hung over the back and I could see the bloodstained tongue hanging out and the open eyes staring lifelessly at nothing. I saw it was a chestnut with a long thin neck and a white streak down the forehead.

I think it was Ginger: I hope it was she, for if so her troubles are over and she is at peace.

CHAPTER SIXTEEN
The Election and Afterwards

As we came into the yard one afternoon, Polly came rushing out. "Jerry!" she cried. "Mr Bennett's been here asking about your vote and he wants to hire your cab for the election. He'll come back for an answer."

"You can tell him my cab will be otherwise engaged for I won't have it pasted all over with posters and I won't have Jack and Captain race about from public house to public house to bring in half-drunken voters."

Polly looked worried.

"Don't frown so," said Jerry. "There will be plenty of work on election day."

Jerry was right.

First there was a fat gentleman with a carpet bag who wanted to go to Bishopsgate Station.

Then we were asked by a group of people to go to Regent's Park, and after that a timid little lady asked to be taken to her bank.

We had just set her down when a red-faced gentleman, clutching a handful of papers, came running up, shouted, "Bow Street Police Station," and jumped into the cab.

The streets were very full, and cabs with candidates' colours on them were dashing through the crowd. We saw two people knocked down that day, one a woman.

It was the first election I had seen and I never wanted to see another.

When we found time, Jerry gave me a good meal of crushed oats and bran, and he was just about to eat a pie that Polly had given him when a poor young woman carrying a child came along the street.

She was plainly bewildered, for she looked this way and that as if she was lost. Eventually she came up to Jerry and asked if he could tell her where St Thomas's Hospital was. She told him that she had just come up from the country and had not known the election was on. Just then the baby started crying.

"Poor little fellow," she said. "He suffers so much pain. He's four years old and can hardly walk, but the doctor has made an appointment for him at St Thomas's, to see if he can be treated. How far is it, sir?"

"Why, missus," said Jerry. "You can't get there walking through crowds like this. It's three miles away. You might be knocked down and the child run over. Now get into the cab and I'll drive you there."

"No, sir," she said. "I can't do that. I have only enough money to get home."

"Look here, missus," Jerry insisted. "It's coming on to

rain. I've got a wife and children of my own, and I know how I would feel if they were in your place. Now get in."

"God bless you, sir," the woman cried, bursting into tears.

Just then, two men with a candidate's colours in their hats and buttonholes ran up, calling, "Cab!"

"Engaged!" said Jerry. But the men ignored him, pushed the woman aside and sprang into the cab.

"The cab is engaged by that lady, gentlemen," Jerry said, stern as any policeman.

"Lady!" said one of the men. "She can wait. Our business is much more important. And besides we were first in and it is our right to stay in."

"Stay as long as you want, gentlemen," said Jerry. "I can wait while you rest yourselves." And he turned his back on them and walked up to the young woman.

The men got out, calling Jerry all sorts of names and threatening to take him before the magistrates before they hailed another cab that was passing.

We were soon on our way to the hospital, keeping to quiet side streets as much as possible. When we got there, Jerry helped the woman down and rang the hospital bell.

"Thank you a thousand times, sir," she said. "I could never have got here alone."

"You're welcome," said Jerry. "And I hope your child will soon be better."

The rain was coming down heavily now, and we were just about to go, when the hospital door opened and a porter called, "Cab!"

The lady who came down the stairs stopped when she got to the cab and said, "Jeremiah Barker! Is that you?"

"Indeed it is, ma'am," said Jerry. "Where can I take you?"

"To Paddington Station," she said. "And on the way you can tell me about Polly and the children."

I learned that Polly had been the lady's maid before she had married Jerry and had kept in touch with her over the years.

"And how do you find cab work suits you in winter," she asked after Jerry had told her all about Polly, Harry and Dolly. "Polly was very worried about you last year."

"I did have a bad cough that wouldn't go away," Jerry said. "And Polly does worry when I'm out in all weathers for hour after hour."

"Well, Barker," she said. "There are many places where good drivers and grooms are wanted. And if you ever think you ought to give up this cab work, let me know. And here," she went on, taking some coins from her purse. "There's five shillings each for Harry and Dolly. Give it to Polly for them, she'll know what to do with it."

* * *

Not long afterwards it was Christmas – a very merry

time for some people but not for cabmen and their horses. There are parties and balls to take people to, and so many places of entertainment open that the work is hard and often late.

Sometimes drivers and horses would have to wait for hours in the cold while the people inside dined, danced and played their games, forgetting the weary cabman on his box and his horse standing till his legs were stiff with cold.

Captain was no longer with us – he had become so old and lame that he had had to be put down, which made everyone very sad. The new horse was a handsome five-year-old called Hotspur who had worked for a noble family until he had been so badly scarred in an accident that he was no longer fit for a gentleman's stables.

I worked in the evenings, for Jerry was wary of letting Hotspur take the cold, and I couldn't help noticing how bad Jerry's cough was and how concerned Polly was for him when we got back late at night.

On New Year's Eve we were hired to take two gentlemen to a grand square in the West End. We dropped them off at nine o'clock and were asked to come back at eleven. "But it's a card party," one of them said, "so we may be a few minutes late."

At the stroke of eleven we were at the door, but there was no sign of the men.

By the time the clock struck twelve, we were drenched by driving rain.

Jerry climbed down from the box, pulled my cloths tight round my neck and walked up and down, stamping his feet and beating himself with his arms to keep warm. But this set him off coughing, so he opened the cab door and sat in the bottom, his feet on the pavement.

At half-past twelve, he rang the bell and asked the servant if was to be wanted that night.

"Oh yes," he said. "They will be with you soon."

It was another three-quarters of an hour before the two gentlemen appeared. They got into the cab without a word of apology and told Jerry to drive to an address two miles away.

By the time we got home, he could hardly speak and his cough was dreadful.

"Could you get Jack something warm," he gasped to Polly who was waiting. "And then boil me some gruel."

Despite his shortness of breath, he rubbed me down as usual and went up to the hayloft for an extra bundle of straw for my bed. Polly brought me a warm mash and then they both went to the house.

It was late the next morning when I heard someone come to the stable.

It was Harry.

He cleaned and fed Hotspur and me, but he was quiet

and didn't whistle as he usually did when he helped his father.

He came again at noon to give us food and water, and this time Dolly came too. The poor girl was crying. "I don't want Daddy to die," she sobbed.

Harry tried to comfort her, but he had obviously been crying as well.

Two days passed and the only people we saw were Harry and Dolly, for Polly was always at Jerry's side.

On the third day, the Governor – the driver who had been on the cab stand longest – came to see how Jerry was doing.

"He's very bad," said Harry. "It's something called 'bronchitis', and it will turn one way or the other to-night."

"I'll look in tomorrow to see how things are," said the Governor.

He was back even before it was light to hear the news that Jerry was much better and was going to pull through.

Over the next week or two Jerry slowly got better. The Governor came every day to take Hotspur out in his cab, for he was such a young horse and had so much energy it would be bad for him to be laid off for too long. He gave Polly half of what they earned, which helped to pay the bills.

I heard him tell Harry that a week or two's rest would

do me the world of good, but to take me for a turn up and down the street to stretch my legs.

Jerry grew better and better, but the doctor said he must never go back to work on the cabs again if he wanted to live to a ripe old age. I heard Dolly and Harry talk about how worried Polly was about what would happen to them all and what they could do to earn money

One day when Harry was sponging down Hotspur after he had come in from work, Dolly came into the stable.

"Who lives at Fairstowe, Harry?" she asked. "Mother has just received a letter from there, and she seemed so glad she ran upstairs to Daddy with it."

"Fairstowe," said Harry. "That's the name of Mrs Fowler's place. You know – the lady who gave us five shillings each on election day. I wonder what she wants. Run and see, Dolly."

She was back a few minutes later, dancing with delight.

"Oh, Harry," she cried. "It's wonderful. We're to go and live in a cottage near to Mrs Fowler's house. It's got a garden and a hen house and apple trees. Her coachman's leaving in the spring and Daddy's to take his place. There are rich people all around so you'll be able to get a job as a gardener's boy, or a stable hand or a page, and there's a good school for me. Mummy is so happy she's laughing and crying at the same time."

"Not a page boy," said Harry. "Imagine having to wear all those tight clothes and rows of buttons. I'll be a groom or a gardener."

And so it was settled. As soon as Jerry was well enough, they would all leave for the country. The cab and Hotspur and I were to be sold as soon as possible.

I have never felt sadder, for the time I had spent with Jerry had been the happiest since I had left Birtwick all those years ago. I had been with him for three years, but even with such a kind master as Jerry, they had taken their toll.

One of the drivers bought Hotspur, and I heard that Jerry had said that I was not to go back to cab work with just any old driver. But the Governor promised to find me a new place where I would be comfortable.

I never did see Jerry again after that New Year's morning when we had arrived back at the yard, soaked to the skin. Even when the day came for me to leave, he was still not allowed out of doors.

Polly and the children came to say goodbye.

"Poor old Jack. Dear old Jack," said Polly. "I wish I could take you with us." She laid her hand on my mane, put her face close to my neck and kissed me.

Dolly was crying and kissed me, too, and Harry stroked me a great deal but was so sad he said nothing.

And so I was led away to my new place

CHAPTER SEVENTEEN

Jakes and the Lady

I was sold to a corn dealer whom, the Governor said, Jerry knew. With him, the Governor thought, I should have good food and fair work.

I was well fed, that was true. But as to fair work – I was always being asked to carry more than I should, for frequently when I had a full load, my master would order another sack or two to be put on.

Jakes, my carter, often said it was more than I ought to take, but he was always overruled.

"No use making two journeys when one would do," the dealer would say.

The other thing that upset me was that the drivers all used the bearing rein, which prevented me from pulling easily, and by the time I had been there two or three months it had begun to tell on my strength.

One day, when I was loaded more than usual and I was going up a steep hill, I had to stop several times to catch my breath. This angered Jakes so much that he began to whip me and shouted, "Get on you lazy fellow, or I'll make you."

I struggled on for a few yards then had to stop again.

Jakes began to flog me cruelly, when a lady came over to him and said, "Please stop whipping your poor horse. I'm sure he is doing his best and the road is very steep."

"If doing his best doesn't get this load up, he must do more than his best, ma'am," said Jakes.

"But it's a very heavy load," protested the lady.

"I agree, but that's not my fault. We were just about to set off with what I thought was a full load, when my foreman made me put another three hundredweight on the cart."

He was just about to whip me again when the lady said, "Please stop. I think I can help you if you'll let me."

Jakes laughed.

"He can't pull with his full power," the lady went on. "The bearing rein is holding his head back. If you were to take it off, I'm sure he would do better," she said persuasively.

"Anything to please a lady," said Jakes. "How far should I take it down?"

"As far as you can. Give him his head completely."

Jakes loosened the rein as far as he could. I put my head down as far as it would go then tossed it several times up and down to get rid of the dreadful stiffness in my neck.

"Good fellow," said the lady, patting me on the head.

"Now, if you speak kindly to him and lead him on, I'm sure he will do better."

"Come on, Blackie," said Jakes. And I put my head down and threw my whole weight against my collar. Using every ounce of my strength, I pulled the load steadily up the hill and only at the top did I have to pause for breath.

The lady followed us up. "There," she said. "He was quite willing when you gave him a chance. I am sure he is a fine-tempered creature, although he has probably seen better days. Now you won't use that rein back on, will you?"

"I can't deny it helped loosening the rein like that, ma'am," said Jakes, "but if I went without a bearing rein, I'd be the laughing stock of the stables. It's the fashion you see."

The lady told him that more and more of the gentry had given up using the bearing rein – in fact, her own carriage horses hadn't worn them for fifteen years. "Surely it's better to lead a good fashion than follow a bad one," she went on. "But anyway, I must detain you no longer. Thank you for trying my plan with your good horse." And with another pat on my head, she was off.

"What a lady that was," said Jakes to himself. "She spoke to me as if I was a regular gentleman. I'll try her plan, uphill at any rate."

And he did. Whenever we came to a hill, he gave me my head and I managed them all.

The overloading went on though. And I was getting so tired that a younger horse was brought in in my place and I was sold to a man who had several cabs.

I think I got out just in time, for the corn merchant's stable was a badly lit place with light coming in through just one small window at the end farthest from my stall.

This had started to weaken my sight, and when I was brought out of the darkness into the glare of daylight, it was sore on my eyes. Several times I stumbled over the threshold for I could barely see where I was going.

But fortunately I got away without any permanent damage to my eyes.

CHAPTER EIGHTEEN
Hard Times

I shall never forget my new owner, Nicholas Skinner. He had black eyes and a hooked nose. He had more teeth than a bulldog and a voice as harsh as a cartwheel going over gravel.

I had never known before how terrible a cab horse's life could be, but I did now, for Nick Skinner had a bad set of cabs and a bad set of drivers. He was as hard on his men as they were on the horses, and we worked seven days a week, no matter what the weather was like.

I was driven by a man who used a whip that was so sharp at the end that it sometimes drew blood.

But still I did my best and never held back, for, as Ginger had said, men are our masters and can make us do what they want.

My life was so wretched that, like Ginger, I began to wish I would drop dead at my work, and one day my wish nearly came true.

I had been at work since eight o'clock and had worked hard all day when my driver took a fare to the railway station. After we had dropped them off, we joined the

line of cabs waiting for a return fare. The next train to come in must have been crowded, for all the cabs in front of us were soon taken and we were hailed by a party of four – a tall man, his wife, son and daughter – and a great deal of luggage.

The lady and the little boy got into the cab as the man busied himself organising the luggage. The little girl walked round to the front of the cab and looked at me. "Papa," she said, "this horse cannot take us and our luggage so far. Look at him. He's weak and worn out."

"Oh, he's all right, miss," said the driver. "He's strong enough."

The porter who was pulling some heavy boxes towards the cab suggested that as there was so much luggage perhaps they should take a second cab.

"Can your horse do the job, or can't he?" asked the gentleman.

My driver assured him I could and helped the porter load a box on that was so heavy I could feel the cab's springs start to strain.

"Papa, do take a second cab," the girl urged her father.

"Nonsense, Grace," he said gruffly. "Now get in at once."

My friend had no option but to obey. She climbed into the cab and once box after box had been loaded on to the top or strapped onto the box beside the driver, the

driver jerked the reins, cracked the whip and drove out of the station.

I managed to keep going until we got to Ludgate Hill, when suddenly I slipped and fell so heavily to the ground that the breath was knocked from me. I lay there thinking I was about to die.

"Oh the poor horse. It is our fault," cried Grace, jumping down from the cab.

I felt someone unbuckle my throat strap then someone threw some cold water over me and poured something sweet into my mouth.

Gradually I got my breath back and somehow staggered to my feet. I was led to some stables nearby and given some warm gruel.

Later I was well enough to be led back to Skinner's stables and in the morning the horse doctor came to examine me.

"This horse is badly overworked," he said. "If you could turn him out in a field for six months and make sure he's well cared for, he'll be able to work again."

"I don't have fine fields to nurse sick horses in," said Skinner. "I work my animals as long as they're good for and then I sell them for whatever they fetch, for dogs' meat if I have to."

"There's nothing basically wrong with him," said the horse doctor. "There's a horse sale coming up in ten days.

If you rest him and feed him until then, you'll get more for him than you would at the knacker's yard."

I had ten days of perfect rest, plenty of good oats, hay and bran mash, and was then taken to the fair, which was held a few miles outside London.

I knew that anything would be better than life at Skinner's, so I held up my head and hoped for the best.

CHAPTER NINETEEN

A Happy Ending

I was in poor company – some of the horses were lame, some had lost their wind, some were old, and others were in such poor condition that it would have been kinder to shoot them.

Many of the buyers and sellers were not much better than the beasts they were bargaining for. But there were some men there I would willingly have served. There was one tottering old man who took a great fancy to me, and I to him, but I was not strong enough for him.

I don't know how long I had been there when I saw a man who looked like a gentleman farmer coming from the part of the fair where the better horses were being traded. He had a strong back, a kind, ruddy face and was wearing a broad-brimmed hat.

He stopped and gave me a pitiful look. I pricked up my ears and looked at him. "There's a horse that has seen better times, Willie," he said to the boy at his side.

"Poor old fellow," said the lad. "Do you think he was a carriage horse, Grandpapa?"

"Oh yes," said the farmer. "Look at his nostrils and

ears, the shape of his neck and shoulder. That's a well-bred horse."

The boy stroked my nose. "Could you buy him and make him young again, as you did with Ladybird."

"Ladybird wasn't old," laughed the farmer. "She was run-down and badly used, that's all."

"I don't think this one is old," said the boy. "Look at his mane and tail. And his eyes are not sunk like some old horses."

"The young gentleman knows his horses, sir," said the man who was selling me for Nick Skinner. "He's been overworked on the cabs and I heard the horse doctor say that, given six months in the fields, he'd be as good as new. I've been looking after him these ten days, and I never met a more sweet-tempered horse. It would be well worth paying five pounds for him now, for in six months he'll be worth twenty."

"Grandpa," cried the little boy. "You said the colt you just sold fetched five pounds more than you expected. So you'd be no poorer if you bought this one."

The farmer felt my legs, which were swollen and strained, and then he looked in my mouth. "I'd say he's about thirteen or fourteen. Trot him out for me, will you?" he said to my man.

"How much will you take for him?" he asked after I had trotted as well as I could.

"Five pounds," replied my man.

"Very well," said the gentleman, counting out five sovereigns into my man's hands.

I was led to an inn, given a good feed and ridden gently to my new home by a servant.

Mr Thoroughgood, the man who bought me, ordered that I should have hay and oats, night and morning, and given the run of a meadow during the day.

"I'm putting you in charge of him, Willie," he said to his grandson.

There was not a day from then on that Willie didn't come to see me, often picking me out from the other horses and giving me a piece of carrot, or stroking me as I ate my oats. Sometimes he brought his grandfather, who always examined my legs.

"Old Crony is improving steadily, Willie," he would say. "Well done."

Rest, good food, gentle turf and exercise soon began to tell on me, and when spring came Mr Thoroughgood harnessed me to a light cart and drove me for a few miles. My legs were not nearly as stiff as they had been, and I trotted with great ease.

"He's growing young, Willie," I heard my master say. "By midsummer he'll be as good as Ladybird. We can give him a little work now, and then we'll find him a good home."

"Oh, Grandpapa," cried Willie, "aren't you glad you bought him?"

"Indeed I am, my boy. But he has you to thank more than me."

* * *

One day during the summer, Mr Thoroughgood's groom cleaned and dressed me with such care that I knew something was afoot. He trimmed my fetlocks and legs, polished my hooves and even parted my forelock.

I was harnessed to the carriage and driven to a pretty house about two miles from the village where Mr Thoroughgood lived.

Willie waited in the carriage while Mr Thoroughgood went inside after a servant had opened the front door. A few minutes later he came out with three ladies. One was tall and pale and leaning heavily on a young woman with dark eyes and a very merry face. The third was a very stately looking woman.

"I do not think," said the tall lady, "that I would like to be driven by a horse that has gone down. If he fell again when I was in the carriage, I would never get over the shock."

"But many first-rate horses have had their knees broken through no fault of their own," said Mr Thoroughgood. "What do you think, Miss Blomefield?"

"You have always advised us well about our horses, Mr

Thoroughgood. We'll take him on trial for a week, as you suggest, if our coachman likes the look of him. I'll send him round tomorrow."

The next morning, a young man came and examined me carefully. At first he looked pleased but when he saw my knees he said in a disappointed voice, "I did not think, Mr Thoroughgood, that you would recommend a blemished horse like that to my ladies."

"You're only taking him on trial. And if he is not as safe as any horse you ever drove, send him back."

I was led to my new home and put in a comfortable stable.

The next morning, when the groom was cleaning my face, he noticed the white star on my forehead. "That's just like the star Black Beauty had," he said. "I wonder where he is now."

Then he saw my white foot and the little patch of white hair on my back. "That's what John Manley used to call 'Beauty's threepenny bit'. It must be Black Beauty."

He hugged my neck and cried, "Beauty! Do you know me? Little Joe Green that almost killed you the night you brought the doctor to Mrs Gordon."

I put my nose to him and tried to say we were friends, and I never saw a man look so pleased.

That afternoon I was harnessed to a light carriage and taken to the house.

Joe Green helped the dark-eyed lady with the merry eyes into the carriage and got in alongside her. "He seems like a fine horse, Joe," she said after she had driven me for a few minutes.

"Indeed he is, Miss Ellen," said Joe. "He's Squire Gordon's old Black Beauty."

"I must write to Mrs Gordon and tell her that her favourite horse has come to us," said Miss Ellen. "She will be so pleased."

After this I was driven every day for a week or so, and as I seemed to be quite safe, Miss Lavinia, the tall lady who had been nervous about taking me on, ventured out with me in the small closed carriage.

I have now lived in this happy place for a year. Everyone calls me Black Beauty again, and Joe Green is the best and kindest groom in the world. Willie comes to see me quite often, and one day when he brought his grandfather, I heard Mr Thoroughgood say to Joe that I should live to be twenty, maybe more.

My ladies have promised that I shall never be sold, so I have nothing to fear.

And here my story ends. My troubles are over and often, before I am quite awake, I dream I am still in Squire Gordon's orchard standing with my old friends under the apple trees.